W9-CAJ-844

To my mother, who taught me the love
in a circle of arms,
and to my dad, who taught me how
love's ripples go out and out . . .
thank you with all my heart
—M.T.R.

To the sweetgrass basket women
of Charleston, South Carolina
—E.B.L.

# CIRCLE UNBROKEN

## The Story of a Basket and Its People

MARGOT THEIS RAVEN PICTURES BY E. B. LEWIS

FARRAR, STRAUS AND GIROUX

*Now, you've asked me, child, how I come to sew.*
*Well put yourself in Grandma's arms,*
*and listen to a circle tale,*
*from long, long ago . . .*

Once, your old-timey grandfather lived in a village by a fine flowing river, across a wide, deep ocean, in faraway Africa.

On the hills by the river grew pale stalks of rice to feed the village and the spirits of the land. By the banks of the river grew tall, grassy reeds to weave into baskets to winnow the rice.

One day after harvest, when he was no longer a boy
—but not yet a man—your old-timey grandfather
was led by the men who lived in the village
to a grove in the forest where the palm trees grew.
It was their sacred place—the Poro bush—
not far from the rice and the fine flowing river
where the men beat their drums and a boy became a man.

"Can you bring water in a basket?"
a masked *Spirit* asked him there.
When he answered, "Yes," the men of the village
took him into the grove, gave him a name,
and taught him all they knew.

*Just as I am teaching you . . .*

They taught him to make ropes and nets and traps;
to hunt in the woods, and harrow and hoe;
to make drums from logs to pound as he danced;
and to sew great baskets to hold the rice.

"The basket starts here," they said
and taught his fingers to talk,
to make a knot first. A coil.
A circle unbroken.
Then his basket grew and grew,
circle on circle, coil on coil.
And when his fingers talked just right
and the wet season came—
his basket held the rain,
and the men were pleased.

*Just as I am pleased with you . . .*

But the wide, deep ocean held the rain, too,
and the rain fell bitter as your grandfather's tears
when the slave men came and bound him in chains
and stole him from his village to a ship
bound for a strange new land.

In the port of Charleston he was put on a stand
and heard the auction man cry:
"Goin' fast—goin' slow—goin' high—goin' low."
He was sold to a master who owned a great plantation,
by a long, curving river that flowed to the ocean
that touched the shores of his faraway Africa.

He lived in a shanty shingled with cypress.
He worked in the rice fields from day clean to sun-go-red.
But long night, after long day,
he sewed baskets in the old way,
from the bulrush that whooshed and hushed
by the marshes and the rivers that flowed to the sea.

The grasses brought him comfort.
His fingers knew their secret.
"Never forget," they whispered,
as he sewed palmetto strips
in and out—around and through.
His circle grew and grew.
And when his fingers talked just right—
his basket held the rain,
and he remembered from where he came.

Now, on a nearby plantation lived your old-timey grandmother,
who came, too, from a village across the wide, deep ocean.
Long ago, when she was not yet a woman, but no longer a girl,
the women of the village took her into the Sande bush
—their sacred place—and taught her all they knew.

She learned to grow a garden of cassava and sweet potatoes;
to fish with nets when the river was low;
to winnow rice in a fanner basket,
tossing the grains up, fast and slow.
And she learned to sew small baskets
to hold the treasures of her hut—
ginger, palm fruit, and kola nuts.
And when *her* fingers talked just right,
each coil touched so tight,
her basket held the rain.

One day in the shadow of the Big House,
your old-timey grandfather wed your old-timey grandmother.
They had children, and the babies slept in the sun,
in Moses baskets, while the field work was done.
And when the babies cried,
your old-timey grandmother sang to them
soft as gray moss, low as the going-out tide.

Then those children had children,
and those children, too,
till one day the Yankees came with cannons
sounding, pounding, booming over the land.
"What's coming, Grandma?" the yard children cried.
"Freedom!" she said.

And the lap children watched as a sea
of blue coats went marching, marching by.
While the basket children lay, looking up,
not knowing that everything was changing
like clouds blowin' in the sky.

Now it was the times after slavery,
when your great-great-great-grandfather
worked shares on this land of marsh, sea, and sky,
where the creek beds rose high on the old rice fields,
melting them away like shadows into shade.

He built a boat of wood and took it to the sea,
far past the shores where the sweetgrass grows.
Rowing in, he had fish for his family and fish to sell.
Then, long night after long day,
he told children tales of Br'er Rabbit and Br'er Fox,
till their laughing eyes danced
like sunlight on the water,
stars above the creek.

Your great-great-great-grandmamma heard the stories, too.
Next day, she carried fish and wares
to market in the basket she'd made,
toting her burdens and cares high on her head.

And the circle went out and out:
like the stone that milled their corn,
and the net that caught their shrimp,
and the Ring Shout that praised their Lord.

*Just as I give praise for you . . .*

Then their children had children, and their children, too,
until one day across the great wide ocean, a war began.
The men of the island went away like the tide,
while the women waited and sewed, long night after long day.

When the men came home again,
the bridge builders came, too,
tying islands to land with steel-arching hands.
"What's coming, Grandma?" the yard children cried.
"Tomorrow," she sighed.

And the porch children watched as the bridges brought cars,
and the cars brought people.
And the basket children lay looking up at the sky,
not knowing the old ways were leaving
as fast as the cars passing by.

But some folks at night sat around the lamplight,
showing the young ones the road ahead was
over and through—as new hands talked to old friends:
the bulrush, the sweetgrass, palmetto, and pine.

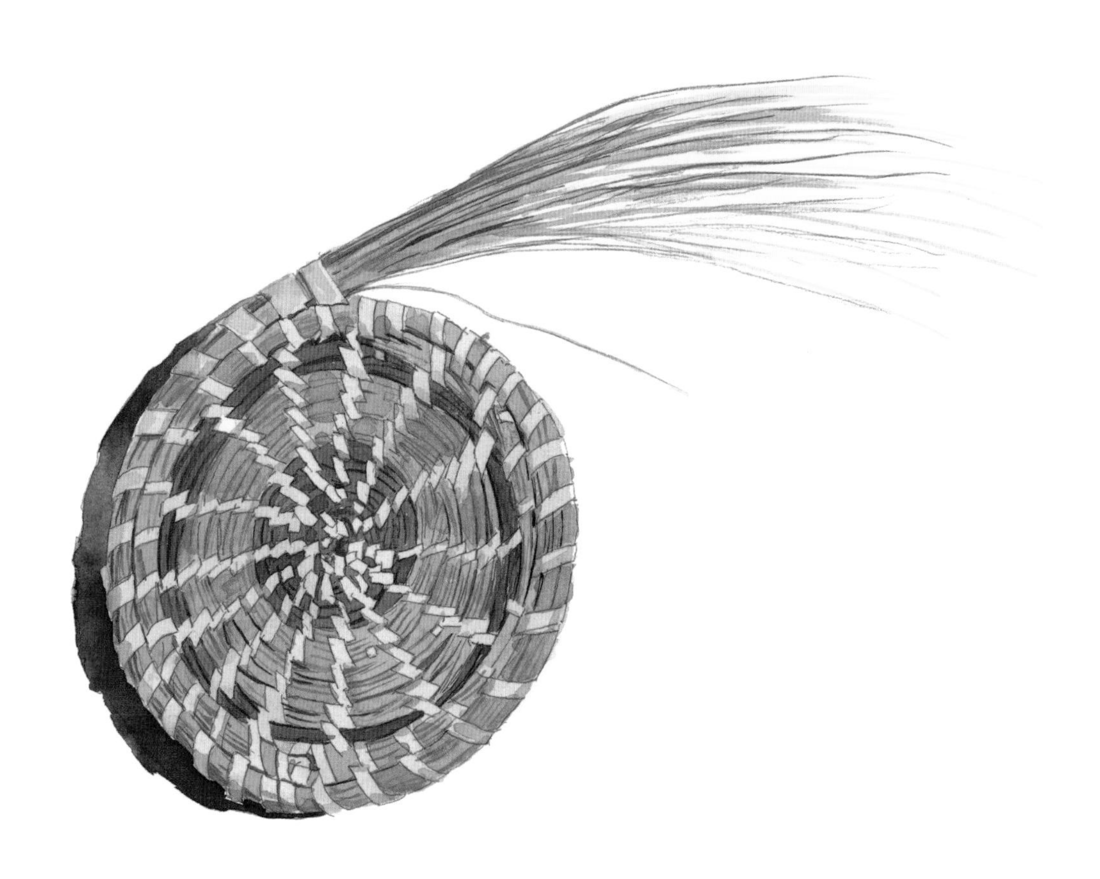

Then those children had children
who put up wooden stands to show their baskets
along the highways and in the marketplace
where the tourists came through—
and thought the beauty of old baskets was something new.

*Just as my baskets are new to you . . .*

While the women sat behind their stands, their sacred place,
sewing and sharing with daughters all they knew,
the men took the boys to *their* sacred place—
the dunes and marshes by the creeks and the sea—
to cut the bulrush, and pull the sweetgrass,
and dry it in the sun as it had long been done.
And so it has always been, time flowing like a river,
circle going out like a pebble in a pond,
until I came along—your mamma—and you.

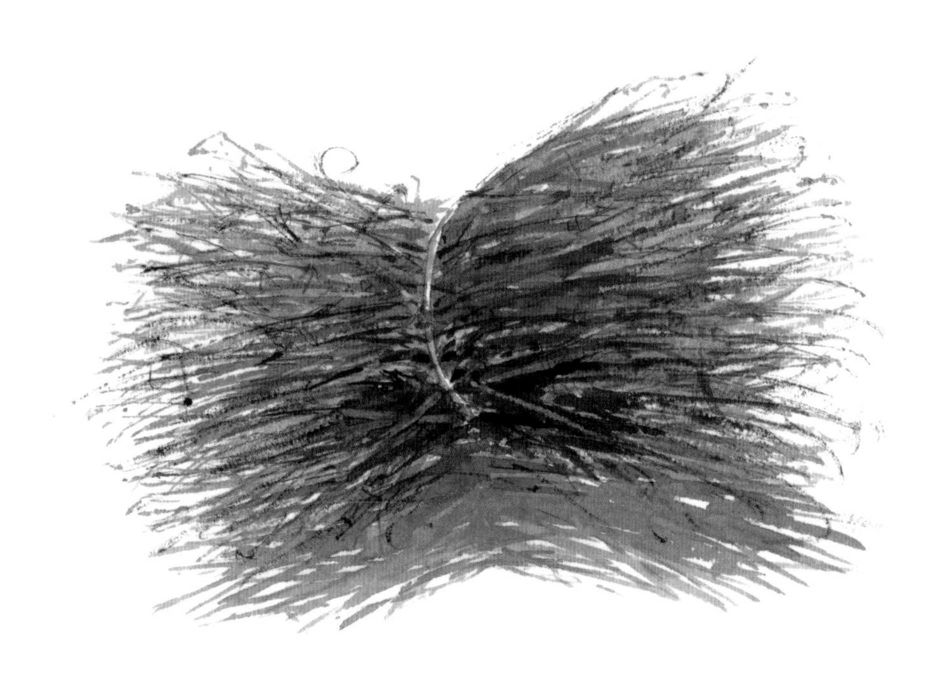

And time has come now, child,
for you to learn the knot that ties us all together—
The circle unbroken.
And when your fingers talk just right
that circle will go out and out again—
past slavery and freedom, old ways and new,
and your basket will hold the past—

*Just as surely and tightly*
*as my arms now hold and circle you . . .*

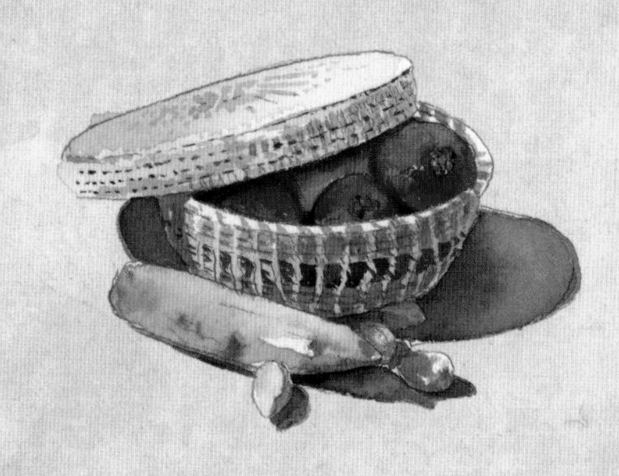

## MORE ABOUT SWEETGRASS BASKETS

The sweetgrass "coil" or "Gullah" basket is truly an ancient art form. Its sewn design traveled to America in the 1700s and 1800s with Africans captured from the Rice or Windward Coast of West Africa by slave traders. Many captives from the region that is now part of the countries of Sierra Leone and Senegal were taken to the Sea Island plantations of South Carolina and Georgia.

On these plantations, a new language called Gullah (Geechee in Georgia) emerged as the dialects of different tribal groups mixed with each other and with English. Tribal skills and customs mixed, too. Coil basketry found a place in the Lowcountry of South Carolina and Georgia, because these coastal barrier islands shared a similar rice culture and sea-grass vegetation with Africa's West Coast.

Though simple in material, sweetgrass baskets are elegant in design. Weavers, or sewers, have passed down their skills from generation to generation. Among Sierra Leone's Mende and Temne tribes, this sharing of ancestral knowledge begins in the Poro bush. Still important today, the Poro bush was both a ruling society of elders and a grove in the forest where young men were initiated into their tribe's culture. The women's bush association was called the Sande. To all, the Poro-Sande bush was sacred and was law.

Usually a young person spent several years in the bush "school" after elders first led the initiate to a palm-leaf-covered door in the forest. With drums pounding, an elder masked as the bush "Spirit" or "Devil" questioned each initiate. One question was "Could you bring water in a basket?" The answer was always yes, because the rain-tight image symbolizes the perfection of the weaver's skill, as row is sewn to row, worked and reworked so closely together that not one gap shows in the finished basket.

Sweetgrass baskets are treasured objects displayed in private collections, exhibits, and museums, including the Smithsonian and the Vatican, but these baskets are more than beautiful art pieces. They are true living history links. Every day, in Africa and America, weavers still sew coil baskets, keeping four hundred years of shared history, pride, and love of basketry alive for new generations; such is the legacy of the circle unbroken.

### ACKNOWLEDGMENTS

The author thanks with deep gratitude the immeasurable contributions the Avery Research Center for African American History & Culture at the College of Charleston, Charleston, South Carolina, made to this book. Thank you in particular to Avery director Dr. Karen A. Chandler, reference archivist Deborah A. Wright, and research assistant Monique Palmer for their readings of the manuscript and their insightful suggestions.

Thank you also to the following facilities for their helpful materials: the Preservation Society of Charleston, South Carolina; the Charleston Museum, Charleston, South Carolina; the Gibbes Museum of Art, Charleston, South Carolina; the South Carolina Historical Society, Charleston, South Carolina; the South Carolina Room, Charleston County Library, Main Library, Charleston, South Carolina; and the McKissick Museum, University of South Carolina, Columbia, South Carolina.

The author especially wishes to acknowledge the Mount Pleasant Sweetgrass Basketmakers' Association, Mount Pleasant, South Carolina, for their guiding spirit in preserving the art of basketry. Lastly, to basketmakers Betty Manigault and Andrea Brown, thank you for your kindness and support, and to my editor, Melanie Kroupa, thank you for your vision and unqualified belief in the subject's worth.

## SELECTED BIBLIOGRAPHY

The following list, selected from almost one hundred sources including books; pamphlets; dissertations; journal, newspaper, and magazine articles; interviews; and videos, is offered for further information about sweetgrass basketry and the Sea Island Gullah culture.

"Basket Making in the Low Country" (Washington Revised Copy). WPA Federal Writers' Project, Charleston County, S.C. South Caroliniana Library, Columbia, S.C.

Branch, Muriel Miller. *The Water Brought Us: The Story of the Gullah-Speaking People*. New York: Cobblehill Books, 1995.

Carawan, Guy and Candie. *Ain't You Got a Right to the Tree of Life?: The People of Johns Island, South Carolina—Their Faces, Their Words, and Their Songs*. Athens: University of Georgia Press, 1988.

Creel, Margaret Washington. *A Peculiar People: Slaves, Religion, and Community-Culture Among the Gullahs*. New York: New York University Press, 1989.

Daise, Ronald. *Reminiscences of Sea Island Heritage*. Orangeburg, S.C.: Sandlapper Publishing Co., 1986.

Fyfe, Christopher. *A History of Sierra Leone*. London: Oxford University Press, 1963.

Jackson, Patricia Jones. *When Roots Die: Endangered Traditions on the Sea Islands*. Athens: University of Georgia Press, 1980.

Joyner, Charles W. *Down by the Riverside: A South Carolina Slave Community*. Urbana: University of Illinois Press, 1984.

Littlefield, Daniel C. *Rice and Slaves: Ethnicity and Slave Trade in Colonial South Carolina*. Baton Rouge: Louisiana State University Press, 1981.

Opala, Joseph A. *The Gullah: Rice, Slavery and the Sierra Leone–American Connection*. Freetown, Sierra Leone: USIS, 1987.

Rosengarten, Dale. *Row Upon Row: Sea Grass Baskets of the South Carolina Lowcountry*. Columbia: McKissick Museum, University of South Carolina, 1986.

South Carolina Folk Arts Program: "Proceedings: Sweetgrass Basket Conference." Columbia: McKissick Museum, University of South Carolina, 1988.

Vlach, John Michael. *The Afro-American Tradition in Decorative Arts*. Athens: University of Georgia Press, 1990.

An Imprint of Holtzbrinck Publishers


For information, address
Square Fish, 175 Fifth Avenue, New York, N.Y. 10010.



ISBN-13: 978-0-312-37603-1 / ISBN-10: 0-312-37603-0

Library of Congress Cataloging-in-Publication Data
Raven, Margot Theis.
Circle unbroken : the story of a basket and its people / by
Margot Theis Raven ; illustrated by E.B. Lewis.— 1st ed.
p. cm.
Summary: A grandmother tells the tale of Gullahs and their beautiful sweetgrass baskets that keep their African heritage alive.
Includes bibliographical references.
[1. Sweetgrass baskets—Fiction. 2. Baskets—Fiction.
3. Gullahs—Fiction. 4. Grandmothers—Fiction.
5. Sea Islands—Fiction. 6. African Americans—Fiction.]
I. Lewis, Earl B., ill. II. Title.
PZ7.R1955 Ci 2004 [Fic]—dc21
2002024009

Originally published in the United States by Farrar, Straus and Giroux
First Square Fish Edition: January 2008
Book design by Barbara Grzeslo
1 3 5 7 9 10 8 6 4 2
www.squarefishbooks.com